FOR

L.C.  T.L.B

tiger tales

5 River Road, Suite 128, Wilton, CT 06897

Published in the United States 2016

Originally published in Great Britain 2016

by Little Tiger Press

Text and illustrations copyright © 2016 Connah Brecon

ISBN-13: 978-1-68010-035-8

ISBN-10: 1-68010-035-1

Printed in China

LTP/1800/1443/0216

10 9 8 7 6 5 4 3 2 1

For more insight and activities, visit us at www.tigertalesbooks.com

PAWS McDRAW

~ THE FASTEST DOODLER IN THE WEST ~

BY CONNAH BRECON

tiger tales

Meet Paws McDraw—
the fastest doodler in the west!

He could draw his way out of *any* danger! He *always* saved the day.

So when the bunnies were in trouble who did they turn to? Paws McDraw!

At the well, Timmy was in trouble. Deep trouble.

Paws pulled out his pencil and started to sketch.

Then he pulled Timmy
up, up, up to safety!

WOO HOO

"Hooray for Paws McDraw!"
cried the bunnies when Timmy
was high and dry.

They carried their hero
home to celebrate.

WELCOME
BUNNY HILL
HOME OF THE
CUPCAKE
POP: ~~656,000,000~~ A LOT!

The bunnies threw a crazy cupcake carnival
in Paws' honor.

(Because y'all know bunnies
LOVE cupcakes, right?)

What an extravaganza of icing
and sprinkles it was! Everyone was
having a rootin'-tootin' time until . . .

. . . in burst
the Rascally Raccoon Gang.

Those lean, mean cupcake rustlers
started tearing up the town!

Paws knew what had to be done.

Someone had to stop the raccoons.

And that someone was *him*.

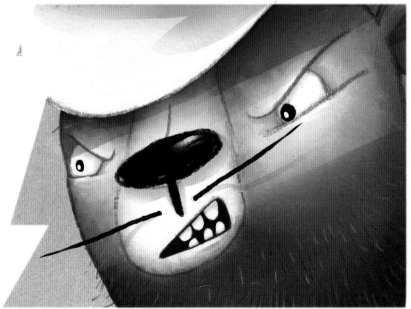

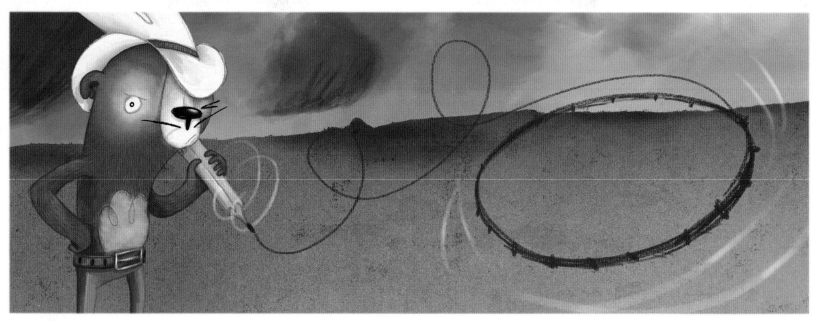

Paws was quick on the draw. He started to doodle . . .

and soon those raccoons were all tied up!

But in the blink of an eye,
they snipped their way free!
Paws needed a new plan. And fast.

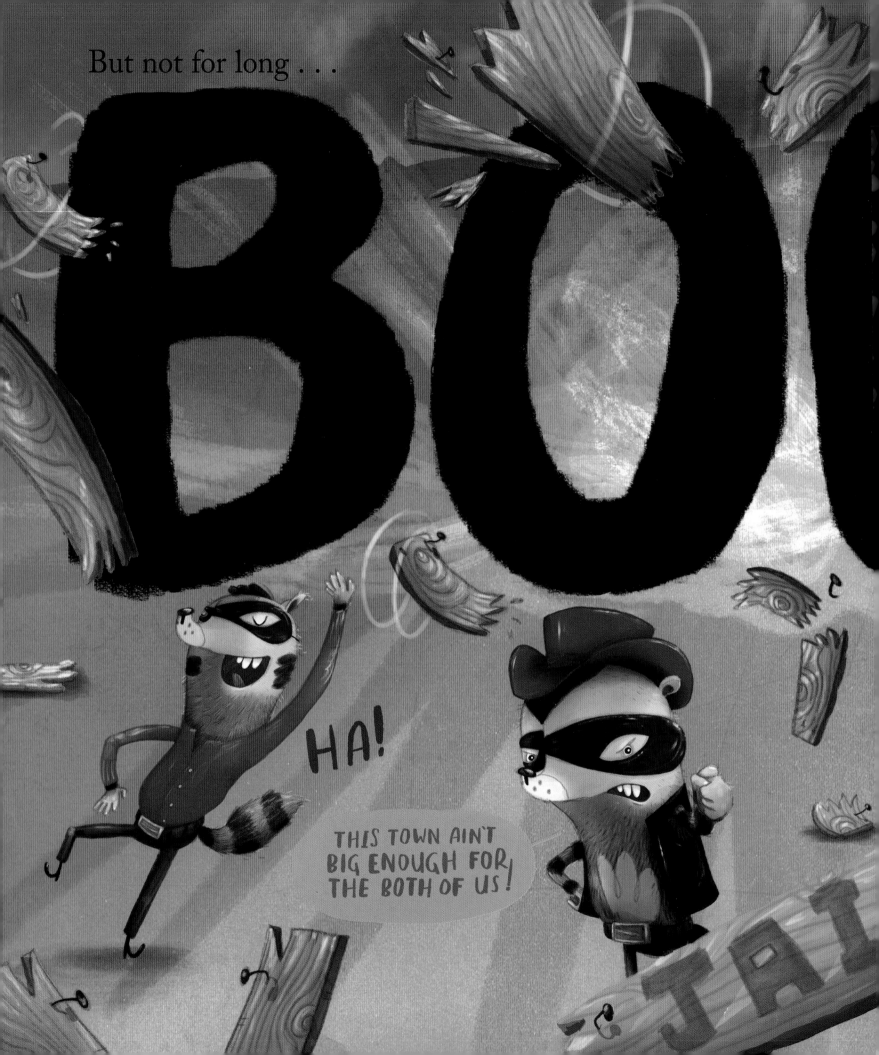

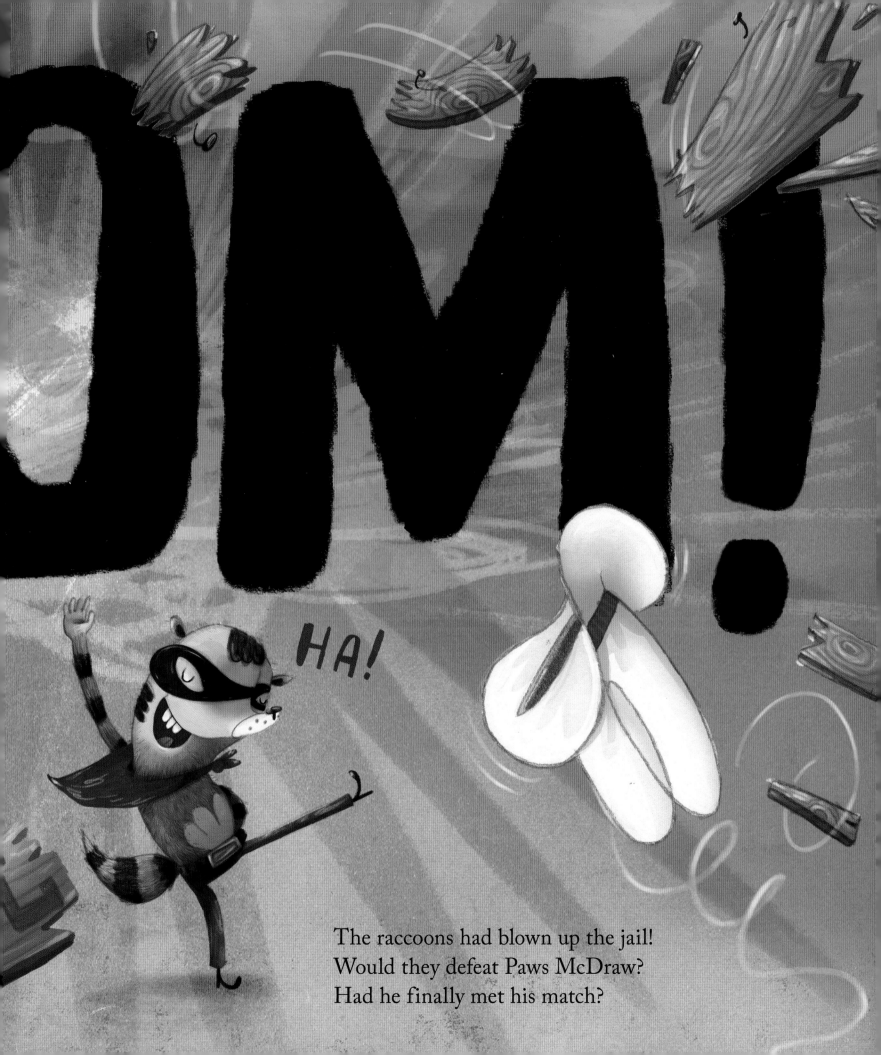

The raccoons had blown up the jail!
Would they defeat Paws McDraw?
Had he finally met his match?

Paws was in real trouble! He was out of ideas! He needed a recipe for success!

And as the baker handed him his pencil, Paws had a brainstorm.

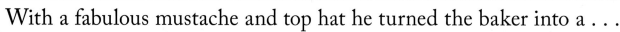

With a fabulous mustache and top hat he turned the baker into a . . .

PRESTO CHANGO!
mix LIGHTLY
HOCUS POCUS!
ABRACADABRA!
BUTTERCREAM
FROSTING
AND
SPRINKLES
ON TOP!

With a swish of his wand and a few magic words, the baker/magician turned those terrible raccoons into . . .

"Woo hoo!" cried the bunnies as they chased the not-so-Rascally Raccoon cupcakes out of town.

Yup, Paws had saved the day again!
(With a little help from his friends.)

Three cheers for the mighty
Paws McDraw!